ORLAND PARK PUBLIC LIBRARY
14921 Ravinia Avenue
Orland Park, Illinois 60462
708-428-5100

DISCARD
OCT -- 2015

To all the kids who love Pete the Cat!
Stay groovy!
Mark 9:23
—J.D. & K.D.

E
Pete
c.2

Pete the Cat and the Bedtime Blues
Text copyright © 2015 by Kimberly and James Dean
Illustrations copyright © 2015 by James Dean
All rights reserved. Printed in the United States of America.
No part of this book may be used or reproduced in any manner whatsoever without
written permission except in the case of brief quotations embodied in critical articles and reviews.
For information address HarperCollins Children's Books, a division of HarperCollins Publishers,
195 Broadway, New York, NY 10007.
www.harpercollinschildrens.com
ISBN 978-0-06-230430-8 (trade bdg.)
ISBN 978-0-06-230431-5 (lib. bdg.)
The artist used pen and ink with watercolor and acrylic paint on
300lb press paper to create the illustrations for this book.
Typography by Jeanne L. Hogle
15 16 17 18 19   PC   10 9 8 7 6 5 4 3 2 1
❖
First Edition

Pete the Cat

and the Bedtime Blues

Kimberly and James Dean

HARPER

An Imprint of HarperCollinsPublishers

ORLAND PARK PUBLIC LIBRARY

Pete and the gang had a great day!
They'd been at the beach. Surf and
sun and tons of fun.

But when the sun went down, they didn't want the fun to end. Pete had an idea.

The party was far-out!
But they knew they couldn't stay up all night.

The gang decided it was time
to say good night.

Pete was just about to catch some ZZZs when . . .

CLAP! CLAP! CLAP!

"Who did that?" Pete asked.

"This cool cat needs to go to bed."

Good night, Gus,

good night, Alligator,

good night, Toad,

GOOD NIGHT,

TIME TO SLEEP!

HOT PIZZA

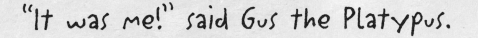

"It was me!" said Gus the Platypus.

"I don't want to go to bed. I want to jam instead."

Pete covered his head. "This cool cat needs to go to bed!" TIME TO SLEEP!

686 SO13

ORLAND PARK PUBLIC LIBRARY

Good night, Gus,
good night, Alligator,
good night, Toad,

GOOD NIGHT,

Pete closed his eyes to
catch some ZZZs when
he heard . . .

HOT
PIZZA

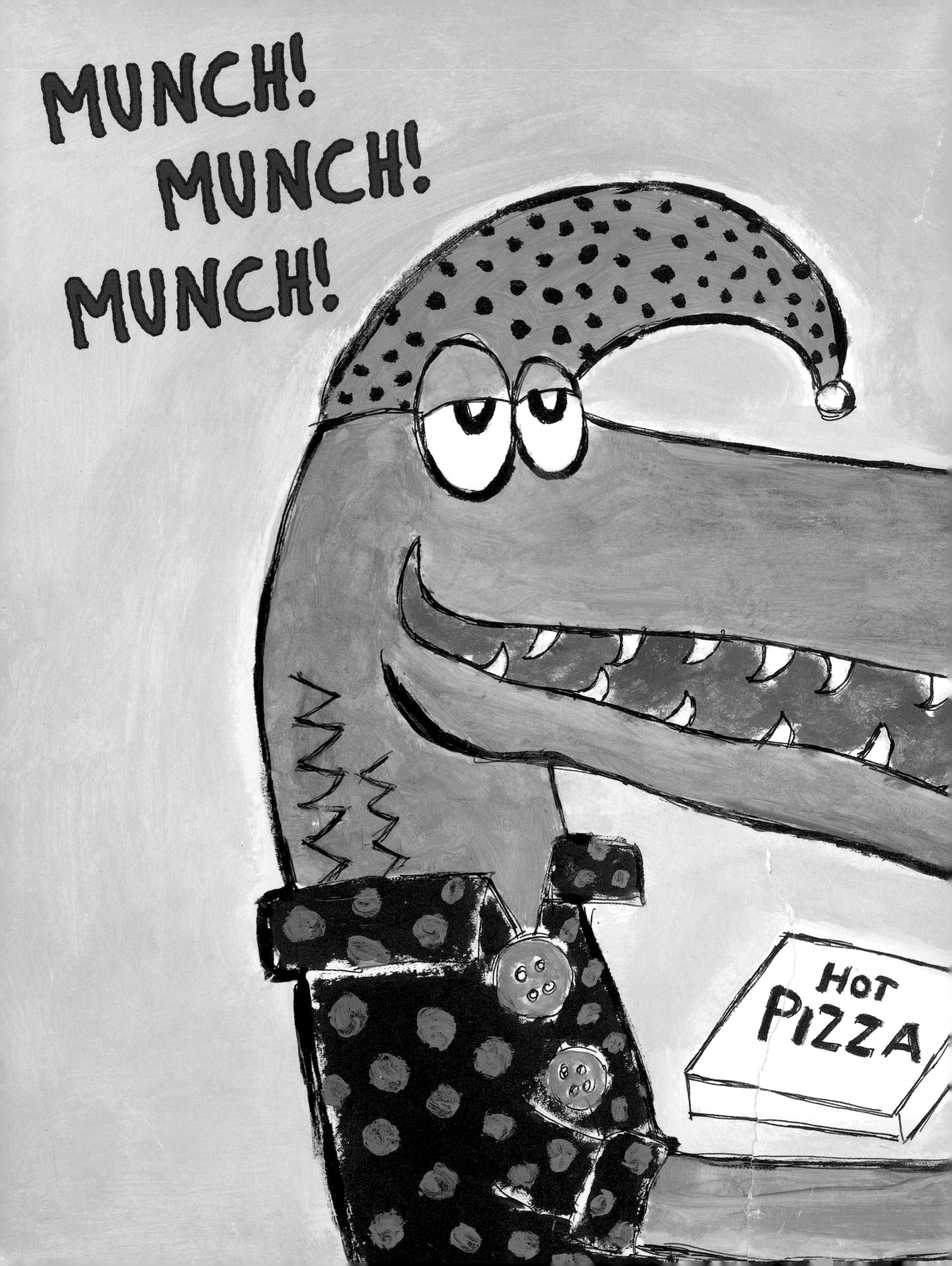
MUNCH!
MUNCH!
MUNCH!
HOT PIZZA

Pete had a hunch.
It was Alligator. He was always
up for eating.

What could Pete do?

All the

CLAPPING,

Rat-A-Tat-Tatting,

and

MUNCHING

was giving him the
bedtime blues.

Pete had a groovy idea.

He got out his favorite bedtime story and started to read—first to himself and then to the gang.

Pete noticed it was finally quiet.

They all settled down.
No one made a sound.

Pete yawned and turned off the light.

"Good night, sleep tight."

Time to catch some ZZZs.

Tomorrow was another day for surfing, sun, and tons of fun.

ORLAND PARK PUBLIC LIBRARY